The Key

A Chosen Novella

Andrea Lynn Ford

CREATIVE FLIGHT PUBLISHING
Newark

Creative Flight Publishing

ISBN-13: 978-0-9890033-9-1

Printed in the United States of America

Book One

No life that breathes with human breath has ever
truly longed for death.

Alfred Tennyson

Arrival

It was a sweltering ninety-seven degrees in Phoenix, Arizona. I loved the hot dry air, and the sun baking down on my skin. I wore my favorite pink cotton sundress to celebrate the beautiful May weather. My social worker picked me up early to head for the airport. I rolled my window down and let the fresh breeze whip my hair about my face. I dreaded going back east. I found it cold and gloomy there. However, there was no point in resisting; I did run away after all. FYI, when you're a minor, and you run away, the authorities tend to frown upon it.

In upstate New York on the quiet shores of Lake Ontario, there is a town named Rochester. It is the kind of town most love. After all, it is an immensely beautiful place filled with history and charm. To me, that town feels like a coffin. It was from that horrid town that I fled several months ago on my trek to nowhere.

"Ami," my social worker said to me, "You cannot do this again. At seventeen, you are old enough to know better!"

To most I look like your average seventeen-year-old girl. I have dark brown shoulder length hair, clear tan skin, and wild childlike brown eyes. Looks can be deceiving though. I am a ward of the great state of New York. I have been most of my life. I am also a permanent resident at Stryker Memorial Hospital.

I have gifts that most people don't desire to understand. I see and hear things that cannot be explained rationally. I seem normal because my personal Hell is trapped inside my head.

"I do know better, but - never mind," I replied. "Don't worry about me. I am going to cooperate this time, and focus on getting better," I lied. Fingers crossed.

I still don't think there is anything wrong with me, or my gifts. I considered them a part of me, but when you are told that you're crazy all of your life, it is hard not to falter. I truthfully expected more of a lecture on the subject before I boarded my plane, but as I got out of the car and set my bag down, she was gone.

✝

It is a six-hour non-stop flight from Phoenix, Arizona to Rochester, New York. Flying is sure to be awful. The close quarters of the plane filled with strangers will undoubtedly overwhelm me. I see and hear way too much on the street let alone packed in a tin can. I guess I should be thankful my social worker didn't stick around to tell the flight attendants of my 'condition'. Who knows, they may have put me in a straight jacket. Instead I slunk into the nearest vacant seat, and blended in with all of the other travelers.

Doctor Borden had been fairly nice about the whole 'escaping' thing. My cross-country trip was behind us. She was pleased that I was coming back on my own accord. She had already alerted everyone of my coming arrival. The angelic Doctor had even acquired me my own private bedroom this time. Doctor Borden's kindness, and the thought of my own bedroom, should have thrilled me, but it just made everything miserable. I wanted nothing more than to be someone else.

My primary motivation for returning quietly, and voluntarily subjecting myself to life with Doctor B at Stryker, is that I refuse to be drugged and forced to be bound. These are two very real possibilities when you are labeled crazy at a hospital.

The Doc met me at my gate and gave me a warm embrace. Surely she was there to make sure I didn't flea again, but it was strangely comforting.

"It is so nice to see you, Amitiel," she said to me as she reached out and took my bag. "You look well. How was Arizona?" The way she referenced Arizona made it seem as though I've been vacationing, and not running from my problems.

"It was fine. I would have liked to stay there you realize," I said rolling my eyes. Seriously, like I want to be a prisoner!

I only had that one carry-on, so we headed straight for the parking lot. A shiver reminded me that my light cotton sundress was not appropriate attire for the cold weather in Rochester. A smile played at the corner of the Doc's mouth as we approached her black SUV. There, lying across the passenger seat was a cream knit sweater. Without a doubt, she brought it for me, as her trench coat covered her floral dress flawlessly. Pleased, I threw it on to get warm, and hopped in.

"I picked up a few new items of clothing for you," she announced happily when we were belted in.

"Really?" I asked surprised. "Like what?" The sweater was a nice touch, but I had to boost the heat. Waiting for her answer I fiddled with the controls.

"For starters, that sweater you're wearing, a few pairs of jeans, some tank tops, and a pair of brown boots. You're a size 7, correct?"

"What is it all for?" I asked astonished. I mean it's not like the Psych Ward was a fashion show or anything. The thought made me even more depressed than I already was. I blew my hot breath on my hands to warm them. My irritation was extremely visible.

She rolled her emerald green eyes at me and smiled, "Do you remember before you – how shall we say… left, when we had lunch together in the rooftop garden, and we talked about trust and responsibility?"

"No, it doesn't ring a bell." Attitude layered thick, I instantly regretted falling back into my old ways.

The Doc didn't even hesitate long enough to acknowledge my poor behavior. "Well, I spoke with your social worker and the hospital board about your situation. We believe that you act out, and take off due to your lack of freedom."

I kind of remembered the lunch, but any conversation that may or may not have taken place evaded me. Thinking about what she said, I was stuck on the word *freedom*. That would explain my lapse in memory. I try to avoid remembering painful subjects.

"We all agree that you might be more comfortable and willing to corporate, if we granted you a few hours each day outside of the confines of the hospital."

I jumped at the comment, "When will this start?" Excitement was growing in the pit of my stomach. All previous thoughts about the cold were long forgotten.

Right away I could feel the shift in the atmosphere of the vehicle. I knew better than to get excited about things. I wanted to kick myself! I could tell from the changing expression on her face that there was more to be explained, and it was the last question she wanted me to ask.

"I've had to do an enormous deal of damage control on your behalf, Amitiel. Your holiday has caused quite a dilemma for me at the hospital. You are *my* responsibility. It reflects poorly on me when you act out, you know. I won't lie to you. While things are better, they are not great. You have disappointed many with your childish actions," she scolded.

"When?" I demanded. My eyes stung with forming tears.

"You may start tomorrow, but…"

But? Oh great! The good Doc waited while I composed my enraged mask into something more serene. The hot tears were free flowing down my reddened cheeks now, and I could taste the blood on my lip from biting it so hard out of embarrassment and frustration.

"As I was saying, you may start tomorrow, but you are to be supervised on your outings. The hospital board feels that after this stunt you pulled hitch hiking across country, only to be found all the way in Arizona, shows your blatant disregard for our boundaries here at Stryker."

"Doctor Borden, I mean Temperance, I don't really think that is necessary. I won't run away again," I mumbled sniffling back more tears. "I promise." I realized that I actually meant what I said. I wouldn't run away.

"Really, Ami, what did you expect?" Temperance asked outraged.

What did I think? Letting this all sink in was harder than it should be. I stared out the window at the birds in the sky. I envied their freedom; the way they glided across the open expanse of the blue sky with little to no effort at all. Soon my eyes dried out. There was no sense in crying like a child. I messed up, big time.

"I already agreed to the condition on your behalf," She said interrupting my thoughts, "...and I would appreciate it if you would make the effort and be good."

She gave me a sideways glance revealing the warm smile on her heart-shaped face. Her eyes sparkled when she smiled. That is how you knew she meant it. Temperance was a beautiful woman. She was probably in her late twenties, with flaming red hair that was layered with rich curls. It bore a stark contrast to her pale white face. Looking at her I couldn't help but smile too.

Temperance didn't always feel distant, like most Doctors. She always mothered me. It was she, who insisted I call her by her first name instead of Doctor Borden. I don't think she is married. The hospital is her life, so that must make us patients, her children.

"You didn't need to do all of this for me." I felt like an ass. "I don't deserve it. I've been difficult." The last part was barely audible.

"I don't mind it in the least. I want you to find happiness here." Her voice caught at the end, acknowledging our approach to the entrance of the hospital.

"Thank you, Temperance. I really appreciate the clothes, and gifted freedom, even if it is supervised." I placed a smile on my worn face. The new tears in my eyes added to the effect, though they were real for a different reason. No need to make the good Doctor suffer along with me. I never did look a kind gesture in the face.

"You're quite welcome, my dear," she said softly brushing a strand of hair from my face.

We chatted a few minutes longer as she flashed her badge to the guards, and pulled into the parking garage. Quickly we left the remaining sunlight behind us driving into the artificial light of the structure. *Home*, I sighed. I found it difficult to reconcile this place as my home, even though it was all that I knew.

The Psychiatric Ward was beautiful of course, there was no belittling that. The walls were a soft therapeutic mint green, and the furniture was all newly updated modern pieces – from the surprisingly comfy chairs in the recreation room, to my impressionistic paintings that hung on the walls. This was all Temperance's doing. She was always finding new ways to cut the budget and divert funds for one project or another. Temperance loved projects. I think that is why she liked me.

We eventually made our way to my new private room. I just stood in the doorway. My mouth gaped when she opened the door. The walls were freshly painted. You could still faintly smell the latex drying. They were a pastel pink, my favorite color, which was far from the usual hospital white. I had a normal bed with a canopy in the corner, instead of the hard-as-a-rock cot on wheels they provide the patients. The linens and duvet appeared to be a cream color, and there was beautiful dark wood furniture added to complete the new bed set. The Doctor outdid herself. This no longer looked like another generic hospital room. It looked as if it belonged in a freaking catalog for interior decorating!

"Where in the world did you find the time or money in your budget for this?" I asked Temperance as she walked past me into the room.

She blushed. "I kind of, sort of, paid for it myself. I don't think I even left here last week. I was excited to welcome you home, Amitiel," she admitted with an accomplished smirk on her face.

I suppose I shouldn't be too surprised. I was the one and only permanent patient here at Stryker. I am a legend among the other patients, and a thorn in every floor nurses side. That thought made me grin. I often found joy in harassing the nurses.

Standing there too afraid to enter and have my new perfect dream of a bedroom disappear, I reminisced about the past. It was hard to believe that still, to this day, no one knows where I came from. Legend says I wandered in the front doors here at the age of seven. Apparently I was rambling about God and Angels. Of course they thought I was completely nuts, especially when I insisted that it was all a mistake, and that I belonged in Heaven with the Angels. This part is a bit murky, but it's what I've been told.

I remember how every news reporter with a camera within a thousand miles showed up that day to film me. The Police were involved, followed by the state authorities, every one of them asking me question after unanswerable question.

No one recognized me or showed up to claim responsibility for me, so I ended up in the system and dropped into the capable hands of Temperance for treatment. It was a blessing in disguise.

Disrupting my heart wrenching flashback, Temperance set my bag down on my new dresser. Turning to me she asked, "Do you approve?"

"Seriously, how could I not?" I exclaimed. "I mean it is over the top, you could say it is flashy even, and you're totally nuts for paying for this yourself, but it is beautiful. I love it," I choked out, overcome with emotion. I was completely embarrassed by her nice gesture. "Why would you do this for me when I ran away?" I finally asked puzzled.

Temperance was thoughtful for a moment before answering me. "I guess I did go overboard," she admitted with an impish grin and a small laugh. "I feel like you're family, Amitiel, and I care for you deeply. You may not like being here, but I would like you to," she paused, "This is your home. Why not make the best of it? I guess I am hoping you'll decide to stick around." She wiped away a tear that escaped down her cheek. Walking towards the door she spun back to me and gave me a quick hug and kiss on the cheek. "Welcome home," she whispered in parting as she exited the room.

Her words hung in the air. Temperance had gone above and beyond for me ever since my admittance ten years ago. She always took an interest in me. I feel terrible for running away, even more so now. I can't believe I didn't think of her, and the mess she'd have to clean up in my wake.

I eventually moved past the doorway, and let the heavy door click shut behind me. I had to admit it was a relief to finally be alone. It was later than I thought. My alarm clock on the night side table read 7:05. Dinner was long over. I could faintly hear the orderly in the hall collecting empty trays. I wasn't hungry, but I had a hard time recalling the last time I ate. Eventually all grew quiet, and I decided to settle in.

After unpacking the few items from my bag, and taking a moment to admire my new wardrobe, I decided to take a hot shower. The water felt nice on my skin. Every muscle relaxed and released tension I didn't even know I was holding. I slowly washed, enjoying the soothing sound the water made as it fell on the hard bathroom tile.

It was not long after my shower that I was cozy and decided that I could not sleep. I wanted to go to the art room and paint. I had privileges most do not around here. Just another perk I suppose, for being Temperance's favorite nut ball.

Everyone should be gone by now, and in his or her own rooms. The thought of quietly painting alone was comforting. I didn't dare venture to the art room during the day. Everyone knew me, and stared at me. Their eyes and thoughts unintentionally burned holes into the back of my head. I was considered a freak because I shied away from human contact. It is a sad fact that even among the disturbed you are judged and labeled.

When I finally approached the doors that led into the art room, I felt a strong rush of excitement. I entered and went straight for my familiar cubby to retrieve my art supplies. There was a blank canvas waiting for me in the center of the room. I sent a silent 'thank you' to Temperance. I'm sure this was her doing. I sat, took a deep breath, my head cleared, and I began to paint.

I never really fit in here. It is really depressing when you can't even find a niche in the Psych Ward. Perhaps my brain is on a different crazy wavelength. The art room is my solace. I've evaded everyone and run here my whole life. My previous assessment was correct. Sitting here alone painting did, in fact, comfort me.

My brush barely left the canvas. Each stroke was more passionate and forceful than the last. I poured my heart out, revealing the artistic use of color attributed to the angel that starred in all of my paintings. Art always soothed me. This painting was one interpretation of many. My Angel artwork lined the walls of this entire floor.

†

I hardly slept that night, even after all the voices in my head were silent. The continuous moans from my neighbor could be heard through the air vent. They grew louder and louder, and did not cease. I buried my head below my soft new pillows in hopes of drowning out the noise. This place could be creepy if you weren't used to it. Sleep evaded me until two in the morning, when I finally heard the floor nurse get off her lazy butt, enter my neighbor's room, and sedate her.

The smell of breakfast and the noise of busy nurses woke me the next morning. I sat up slowly. The memories of yesterday's events flooded my mind. I was still exhausted, but I could no longer rest. After a good stretch, I rose to begin my day.

I took care, happily making my bed. I loved my new surroundings. I parted the curtains to my third floor window, and slid open the glass to let some crisp, fresh air in. My last room didn't have a window at all. In fact, most rooms on this floor don't. I guess Temperance decided I was not at risk for jumping. I smirked.

I picked through the clothes in my dresser finally settling on a light blue tank top, form fitting denim jeans, my new sweater and boots. They fit perfectly. While throwing my hair up in a sophisticated bun, I heard a rap on my bedroom door.

Removing the bobby pin from between my teeth I yelled, "I'll be right there!"

I reached the door as it began to open. I paused, just inside the doorway stood an unbelievably gorgeous visitor. I honestly figured after ten years here that I knew everyone. *He must be new*, I thought.

"Sorry, Miss," he said apologetically as he prepared to back out. "I was just bringing you your breakfast. I'm Buer, by the way. You can call me Bow." Completely abashed for entering uninvited he lowered his head.

"Pleased to meet you, Bow, I'm Amitiel. Everyone here calls me Ami. I'm sure they told you about me," I said with a wink trying to lighten his mood.

This seemed to further his discomfort.

"It's okay. I know you were warned about me." I casually extended my arm to block his exit.

He smirked and lifted his head in response. The moment our eyes met I felt as though I recognized him. This baffled me to no end, because obviously he was different, and we had never met before. There was something about his deep-set hazel eyes. They appeared to have gold flecks that contracted as they captivated my attention.

The longer I stared, the more apparent his discomfort became. He cleared his throat. I give him credit for not yelling for help. I diverted my attention to the food tray in his hands.

"I brought you some oatmeal, fresh fruit, and a hot coffee. Your floor nurse instructed me to do so. She thought you might have had a rough first night back," he said with a bashful smile.

"Could you please set the tray near my bed? The food smells wonderful."

"Of course, Miss," he mumbled as he passed me, and did as instructed.

I blushed a deep crimson. "Ami, please. Just call me, Ami."

Bow raked his left hand through his disheveled light brown hair. He appraised my outfit with a curious look. In good spirits, Bow quietly moved past me and returned to the door. Softly he mumbled, "Do have yourself a good morning, Miss Ami." He returned his hand to his pocket, and disappeared down the outside hall.

Miss Ami, I thought with a giggle.

First Outing

Walking the halls of Stryker Memorial Hospital's Psychiatric Ward takes courage. It seems as though you could find every form of mental disorder residing on this floor.

There are schizophrenics who are typically held in the padded room for fear they'll hurt themselves, and a few quiet socio-paths that give you the creeps simply by looking at you with those cold and calculating eyes. There are those with bipolar disorder, who seem to be normal, but need constant supervision and scheduled medication, and I can't forget the individuals with multiple personalities. They often are entertaining.

There are moans, screams, and incoherent ramblings that flood the hallways at all hours of the day. A simple trip down the corridor to the rec area can feel like a journey of a thousand miles.

I may be well known around here, but the names of those around me change all of the time. The urge to remember a nurse's name, a certain orderly, or even the patient in the next room evaded me, until I met Bow.

From the moment I laid eyes on him he became the focus of every thought that entered my mind. I have this deep intuition that somehow we are connected. I fear that I must keep my distance from that man if I value my remaining sanity.

Temperance was in her office. I could tell from the classical music that drifted from the loud speaker. It was her belief that it would promote inner peace for those who are troubled. I dropped my empty breakfast tray on the nurse's desk, giving the male nurse a sweet smile. It must have worked, he took it, and grinned in return.

Temperance's office was at the end of the main corridor. In order to survive the overload my senses endured here during the day, I ran. I skirted around the corner that led to her office with such speed that I almost smacked right into her closed door. *How odd*, I thought. *Her door is never closed.*

It took a moment to catch my breath, and right myself before knocking. Some how it felt wrong to knock. In all these years, I had never had to.

The door swung open after the first knock. The breath I had unknowingly been holding escaped in an audible whoosh. Unexpectedly the person who opened the door wasn't

Temperance, but rather my gorgeous visitor, Bow.

Bow smiled. "Miss Ami," he said with a slight nod of his head. "Please come in. Doctor Borden has been awaiting your arrival."

I must have looked remarkably lost. I stood there gawking awkwardly at him for several moments. Eventually I gathered my dignity enough to stutter, "H-H-Hello, Bow. Why th-th-thank you."

"Ami, my dear, I see you've met Buer," completely abashed, she caught herself and corrected, "Bow, I'm sorry. You've met Bow, our new Recreation Coordinator."

"Sure, I met Bow this morning. I had no idea who he was though. No offense, Bow," I backtracked. "The turnover rate on employees around here is appalling. I hardly bother with getting attached to anyone," I said flippantly. *Yeah, that will chase him away*, I mentally kicked myself. I go from a stuttering idiot to a bitch, in like thirty seconds. I sighed. My stomach was filled with butterflies.

"That's okay, Miss Ami," he laughed. "I'm fully aware of the issues here. I plan on sticking it out," he grinned.

Was I imagining the exchange of glances between Bow and the Doc? It sounded like he was referring to me, and not his employment situation.

"I'm glad you arrived when you did, Ami. Please have a seat," she said gesturing with her hand to the loveseat that sat opposite from her desk. "Bow, would you take a seat as well? This involves you both."

Following instructions Bow took the empty seat beside me. It was too close for my comfort. Our thighs grazed when he sat. Fidgeting, he began to adjust the pillows for comfort. *Oh great*, I thought. *He told on me. What a coward.* I didn't *entirely* mean to freak him out this morning.

Temperance cleared her throat. "Amitiel," she began.

"Yes?" I replied. By now the tension had my butterfly filled stomach, doing flip-flops. I felt like being sick.

"Bow has volunteered to be your official chaperone on your daily outings." Excitement colored the atmosphere around her.

That did it. My jaw dropped. I was sure I had walked into a trap. So much for being able to rely on my gifts of reading people. What was it with the guy that had me wigged? Hiding my inner angst, I turned my attention to Bow waiting for him to speak up.

"I'm new here, and I would like to get to know you, Miss Ami. Doctor Borden has explained your situation to me. I would like the pleasure of escorting you this afternoon. All I ask in return is for you to show me the ropes."

In a side bar to me he whispered, "I hear you're a celebrity around here."

I was lost in my own head for the moment. Was this guy serious? A celebrity? So Temperance filled him in, hunh? *About what*, I wondered. I couldn't help but want to decipher what *situation* he was referring to. Was it my mental situation? Perhaps it was my ward of the state with no known past situation? Or was it my newly awarded freedom that made him curious? The longer I remained quiet compiling question upon deluded question, the more nervous Bow got. When he began fidgeting again, only this time with the frayed edge of his denim jacket, I figured it was time to answer.

I averted my attention to Temperance and asked, "What are the rules, how long do I have, and are there any boundaries? I'd really like to know the conditions before I answer Bow," I articulated, very proud of myself for sounding strong and confident versus outrageously confused and flustered about the turn of events.

Temperance gave a soft laugh and smiled at the both of us. "Bow would be responsible for your, how do I say... safe keeping. You may have two hours per day, unless otherwise authorized by me, and I would prefer you to remain close, meaning within Rochester. However, I would have to trust the discretion of your chaperone," she gestured to Bow. "Have I answered all of your concerns?"

I nodded not trusting my voice. Strangely I could feel tears in my eyes. Not even sure of their origin, they began to quietly fall down my cheeks. Bow looked at me alarmed. He attempted to grab my hand I'm sure to provide some comfort, but I pulled away. He settled for grabbing a tissue from the box on the table in front of us, and handing it to me. I took a moment to wipe my tears, and organize my thoughts.

My mind never did rest. It was part of my problem. My head was always filled with strange voices, brightly colored auras of those around me, and my own personal thoughts analyzing all of the above. Rest was near impossible. That is why Temperance introduced me to art. Art soothed me. Painting always quieted the voices. My emotions ran high. I felt everything so deep. That is my only conclusion to these strange tears of mine.

"Thank you for the tissue," I sniffed.

Bow, afraid to upset me further, nodded in response.

"I'd like to accept your offer. I could use the air," I said with a pathetic self-loathing, quiet laugh. This was my great attempt at lightening the dour mood I created.

Temperance clasped her hands together pleased, a bright smile lighting her stunning soft features. She rose from her desk and came around to the sofa, where Bow and I continued to sit. She patted my knee with a loving look in her eyes. Bow stood to shake her hand.

"Thank you, Bow. I'm sure Amitiel will be ready to go soon. I'll send her to find you when we finish up here," Temperance said with gratitude. She then saw Bow to the door.

I rose from the loveseat already feeling less overwhelmed in the absence of Bows presence. I crossed the room to Temperance and did something that was out of character for me – I gently grabbed her arm to spin her towards me, and I hugged her tightly. It felt odd to be the one to initiate the hug, but I didn't let go. I justified my actions by acknowledging that Temperance is the closest thing I have to a mother. Children hug their mothers for comfort all the time, I'm sure of it.

For once she had to be the one to pull away. Smiling kindly at her I sniffled, "Thank you."

That did it. Temperance was so shocked and pleased by the hug, that my 'thank you' sent her right into hysterics. Through her laughter she attempted to speak.

"I didn't think it was ever going to be possible. After all this time I began to doubt that I would ever get through to you. I am though, aren't I?" Quieting her laughter she took on a more serious tone. "This is probably deemed unprofessional, but I must explain how much I care for you, Amitiel. I have had the privilege of watching you grow up, and I want you to know that I am proud of you, and well… I love you."

I stood before her with a shocked, absent look on my face.

"Do you understand that, you beautiful, stubborn girl? You are the closest thing I have to family."

"I didn't mean to take you off guard with the hug," I joked. "I may not always show it, but I l-l-love you t-to," I finished, quietly looking down. I felt a shift inside myself. My chest felt warm, and my breath caught in my throat. Raising my head, I smiled at her, and left the room feeling loved.

†

Back in the confines of my bedroom I waged a war with myself over the decision I made to be alone with Bow. My instinct screamed it was a bad idea, but he intrigued me. His eyes held something I still can't rightfully define. This continued for the better part of an hour. Looking at the clock, it read 11:48 in the morning. Intrigue in the end won the debate, and I quickly left my room to find him.

I didn't have to go very far. I practically ran him down in the hallway with my haste. His strong arms reached out and caught me, as the room whirled in response to my sudden stop. When he touched me, I got a mirage of visual clips almost like a movie that played in my mind. I froze and freaked out. It happened too quickly to understand.

"Steady, Miss Ami. I was on my way to spring you," Bow said with a heart-stopping wink. "Care to join me for lunch?" All traces of the earlier awkwardness were gone now.

I decided now was not the time to display how nuts I really am by asking him if he saw the clips too, so I stored the information from my recent hallucination in the back of my mind for future review.

It took me a moment to gather my composure before responding. "I was in a hurry to find you as well, Bow. Sorry about almost plowing you down. I must look crazed to you. This is a Psych Ward after all," I joked lightly.

I was not prepared for Bows reaction. He dropped my arms so quickly, that I felt stung by his rejection. The hard look on his face told me that I had crossed a line, I just wasn't sure which one. He is hot one minute and cold the next. His mood swings were giving me whiplash. It was extremely frustrating how sporadic my readings on him were. It was starting to seem as though he knew I was doing it, and could block me.

"You should not joke about those who are unfortunate, Miss Ami," he reprimanded.

"I'm sorry if I offended you, but I was clearly referring to myself and the current situation I am in," I tried to explain. I pointed to the sign on the wall that read: **Psychiatric Ward, Be Cautious.**

Bow grabbed my hand and looked deep into my eyes. "You're not crazy," he stated earnestly, and then pulled me toward the elevator.

Once in the elevator it felt too close for comfort again. He was still holding my hand, and it felt intimate. I took it back, and decided to ask him what his deal was. Before I had the chance the doors opened, and we were in the lobby. A man in a dark coat was in such a hurry to take our place in the elevator, that he nearly pushed me down. *What an asshole*, I thought.

Bow disrupted my terrible thoughts with his mumbling, "Subconsciously everyone was, of course, fearful that he himself would go nuts – everyone with the exception of those who had already gone nuts, who were in the wholly pleasant situation of having no fear." Bow spoke quietly under his breath to no one in particular. The beautiful serene smile on his face could make Angels weep.

God, his eyes called to me. Was he trying to apologize? Was he flirting?

"E.E. Cummings… It is one of my favorite passages. Do you care for his writing much?" I asked.

No response. We were in the parking lot staring at his motorcycle now, and preparing to leave. Just then it dawned on me, I had no idea where he was taking me. Stranger danger one-oh-one, know where you are, and where you are headed.

"Excuse me, Mr. Cool," I said with an attitude. "Just where in the Hell are you taking me?"

The word Hell caught his attention.

"To lunch."

"Where exactly are we dining?" I began to tap my foot expressing my irritation with his short answer.

Bow spun on a dime, took one look at my childish pouting and burst out laughing at me.

"Seriously?" He asked when my demeanor didn't change. "Okay, okay. I'm taking you to my favorite burger joint down by Charlotte Beach."

When I still looked unhappy and confused, he forcefully yanked me on to the back of his bike without further discussion and sped away.

"Jerk," I mumbled.

†

The burger joint, as Bow called it, was nice. The food was delicious, and the chocolate milkshake stole my heart. Sipping deeply I decided it was time to get to know Bow.

"How old are you?" I blurted out.

Between bites he said, "I'm eighteen."

"You're young. Why do you want to work with us crazies?" I asked, forgetting that using the word crazy might offend him again.

"For the last time, you're not crazy. I chose this job to help people, and to feel good about what I do with my life."

There was a dark undertone to his statement that I didn't fully understand. What could he have done in his short life that would make him feel he needed to repent?

Confused yet pleased with his answer, I continued my interrogation.

"Why the nickname, Bow?"

"I... *hunt*," he said flashing the tattoo of a bow and arrow on his forearm. "My turn to ask you a question now."

I nodded approval returning to my milkshake.

"Why do you think you are crazy?"

That caught me off guard. I mean, on the one hand I really don't think that I am, but hearing voices, seeing auras and having a deep overwhelming intuition is all too much to explain and *not* be touched. Bow was staring at me. I could tell he was watching me sort it all out. I swear I feel like he can see through me. My face must give it away. Oh for Heaven's sake...

"I don't," I blurted out.

"I didn't think you really did," he said popping the last bite of his burger in his mouth.

Bow made a point to stack our empty dishes neatly on the end of the table politely for the waitress, before heading over to the register to settle our bill. After paying, he returned to our table where I remained and laid a large tip down. He gently took my hand.

"We still have some time. Would you like to walk the pier, Miss Ami? Your wish is my command," he said with an exaggerated bow like an early century gentleman.

I couldn't help but giggle. "Why of course," I replied in a thick southern accent playing the role of a proper lady.

Outside the diner, the sun shining brightly made the sixty-degree weather feel much warmer than it was. I took off my sweater and tied it around my waist. The lake-chilled air on the pier was refreshing. I watched the seagulls bounce along the rocks that lined the wharf looking for lunch. It was nice to be out of the hospital.

I turned and began appraising Bow. He had on beige cargo pants, and a gray, extremely fitted worn t-shirt that was topped with a denim jacket. His motorcycle boots turned his style from Old Navy model to sexy badass. Damn he looked amazing.

I must have let my gaze linger too long. He sensed my eyes on him... He stuffed his hands in his pockets and began to flash a wicked grin that showcased his dimples.

"Like what you see?" He asked, tilting his head to the side, dimples still in full effect. He began to wag his eyebrow up and down, mocking me.

I pretended to toss hair over my shoulder with a snotty attitude you only see in cheesy eighties movies muttering, "Please."

Thank goodness! For once I didn't offend him. He actually laughed, but something was off. Bow kept glancing over his shoulder with an odd look on his face. Befuddled could describe his expression. It immediately caught my attention.

"What's wrong?"

"I just have a funny feeling something is not right. Call it my intuition." Sensing my alarm he backtracked, "I'm sure it's nothing."

Now *my* intuition flared. His aura proved he was lying. There was something to be worried about. Now I knew there was danger. My body began to react. Fight or flight.

Quickly, without much thought, I pulled my hair out of the bun and let my waves cascade down hiding my features. Next, I went to put my sweater back on. During which time I cast a glance over my shoulder as I slipped my arm in. That is when I saw him. It was the stranger from the hospital lobby, the man in the dark coat who nearly toppled me over. Instantly I knew, *he* was the danger.

The strange man was following us. I knew it was not a coincidence. The stranger's expression was hostile. Bow couldn't deny the danger any longer. He knew I noticed the man following us. We were quickly approaching the end of the pier where the lighthouse stood. If we continued, there would be nowhere to go, and we would be trapped. We had to act now.

I looked up at Bow with panic written all over my face. He winked, knowing that the stranger was close enough to overhear any plan of evasion we discussed. *He must have a plan*, I told myself trying to soothe my fears.

Bow did have a plan, too. So quickly, that I barely felt the motion, Bow had me pinned up against the lighthouse. He gently swept the hair from my face. Gazing into my alarmed eyes, he slightly nodded towards our pursuer who gawked at us incredulously.

Taking it one step further Bow placed himself against me. His legs spread straddling mine where I stood. He slowly leaned forward, cautioning me with his eyes. My mouth watered in response. I wanted him to kiss me, and I was sure he knew it.

Bow took my face between his strong calloused hands and kissed me. The kiss was gentle at first, but then deepened into pure lust. The moments that led to him kissing me were almost as pleasurable as the kiss itself. He was a good kisser, not that I have any experience to reflect on, I realized.

To the other people on the pier, we appeared to be young lovers. What neither of us foresaw was the effect the kiss had on us. In that instance the entire world around us disappeared. More images invaded my mind. Images of Bow and me tangled in sweat and passion. At a certain moment during the kiss, it almost felt like Bow and I were floating. I could feel his arms wrapped around me tightly, and the tenderness of his warm soft lips moving against mine. Our minds became one... Oh crap! Our minds became one!

It startled me right out of our make believe kiss. Bow froze sensing my discomfort for the wrong reason. All thoughts and worries I had about the angry man following us were long gone. My mind could only process Bow. He became all I could see, and now was another voice in my head that I could hear.

When I finally gathered my wits about me, I noticed that our pursuer had vanished. We took our time heading back down the pier. Both of us were lost in thought.

Mystery

One of best quotes in the world comes from Coco Channel; 'In order to be irreplaceable, you must first be different from the rest.' I often consoled myself with that quote. After yesterday's events, I cannot help but wonder if life would be better if I was ordinary... For once it would be nice to be normal, and if that meant that I was replaceable, I think I could live with that.

I was in my room impatiently awaiting the arrival of Bow. He had nervously taken me back to Stryker yesterday afternoon. If he had his way, he would have taken me someplace else entirely. His parting words still rang clear as a bell in my head. "Breakfast, your room, nine, be ready." So here I was, dressed casually in black fitted pants and an ivory silk top ready and waiting.

The clock read 8:48. Each minute seemed to last a lifetime. My foot dangled off my bed swinging back and forth impatiently. I was tempted to bite my nails, but thought better of ruining my nail polish. Where was he? I'm not exactly sure what to think about the new voice I collected in my head. It has never transpired that way before. Of course I haven't ever kissed anyone before either. The kiss. My mind suddenly was lost reliving that moment.

The door to my room opened without as much as a knock. I knew it was Bow who entered, I could hear him in my head. He was worried, well scared would be a better description. Bow was beginning to suspect that my gifts were far more advanced that he had hoped. He seemed to know me. I found that odd. I suppose it is rude to riffle through someone else's head.

"I'm ready as you requested," I said, figuring that I should do my best not to listen to his private thoughts.

His smile was sweet. "Good morning, Miss Ami. I thought that for today's outing, we could request an hour more of time from Doctor Borden. What do you say?"

"Sounds good to me. What did you have in mind?"

Bows aura had a beautiful array of colors. At the moment, he was a shimmering blue, which stood for loyal and creative among other things. He was a good man. Of that I was sure. The longer he was close, the harder it was to ignore his thoughts in my head. There were things he wanted to tell me, but he was unsure of how I would react. He wanted me to trust him, and he was scared that he would lose it if I knew the truth.

"I was thinking that we could go to Church. It is Sunday after all."

"Well, I suppose there is a first for everything," I replied with a shrug of my shoulders. I hopped off my bed and took my place by Bows side intertwining my fingers with his. "Let's go ask Temperance."

Getting permission from Temperance was an easy task. She seemed quite pleased with the blossoming relationship between Bow and I. At first I was scared to hold his hand in front of her. Bow told me that our display of affection would be fine. He explained that while he was technically employed by the hospital, Temperance had intended our relationship to happen. She knew Bow for many years and would only trust him as a guardian for me.

Bow did make me feel safe. His thoughts and intentions were pure. After the unexplained danger we faced yesterday, I undoubtedly trusted him. I unequivocally had to be with him.

✝

Bow took me to a beautiful old Catholic Church on the outskirts of Rochester, in a suburb called Greece. The architecture of the building was timeless. The facade was entirely made of stone. Gargoyles eerily protected the structure from the eves.

As we walked inside I could feel peace seep into my soul. Mass was over. The Priest was talking with a few remaining parishioners. Bow led me down the red carpet lined isle to a pew in the middle. We sat in silence.

I never did find the silence Bow seemed to have. It troubled me to hear his prayers. It felt like a violation of his trust. So I began distracting myself with the scenery. Behind the pulpit, there was a stained glass wall. It was nearly noon by now, and the sun was high in the sky casting pale yellow rays through the window. The light unmasked the picture the glass contained.

I've always considered myself spiritual, but never religious. Without guidance it is difficult to understand the many forms of religion there are, but sitting here admiring the detailed glass I felt that I understood more than most people do.

"I brought you here for a reason," Bow began. "I'm not exactly who you think I am. The world is not entirely as you perceive it, Miss Ami."

"I have to admit, you're scaring me. Are you some sort of serial killer? Are you going to make a flesh suit out of me?" I said in mock horror.

Bow was not pleased. I didn't even need my gifts to figure that one out. He simply dropped his head in his hands. I felt a wave of mixed emotions flow off of him.

"Could we be serious please?" He asked exasperated. "I have things to tell you, things that affect your future, our future."

"Okay. I'll listen, Bow."

"I have a story to tell you. It is my story. As I said, I am not who you think I am, and neither are you. In order to understand this, I must start from beginning."

"Like when you were a baby?" I didn't see how any of that was relevant, unless we were related…

"Don't get confused, silly girl. Not the beginning of my life or yours, I'm referring to the beginning of time. Do you understand what I am saying?"

"Yes, please continue," I replied taking him more seriously.

"Every life, every soul has a destiny. A clear ending that is already written before you even begin. The path to finding your destiny is the only unclear part. That is because of free will." Bow stopped and asked, "Have you heard of free will before?"

"Yes. Free will is a certain freedom. A sort of self-government, I suppose. It is the right we have to make choices." I wasn't even sure I made sense, but he seemed proud. His thoughts were positive.

"Free will is essentially the greatest unwritten law there is. Not city, state, or even governmental law, it is a universal law."

"Are you referring to God, and Heaven?" I asked, interrupting him.

"I am. You know my name is Buer, and that I prefer Bow. What you don't know is why. I guess you could say I am ashamed of my past, my very extensive past, that is. You see..." he began, pausing to sigh in despair. "Amitiel, I need to know that what I'm about to tell you will not have you look at me differently. I need to know you will use your gifts to know I am being sincere and honest with you."

"You know about my gifts?" I asked shocked. "I was going to tell you, I swear. I just could not afford to have you look at me the way everyone else does."

"I know about your gifts because all Angels posses gifts."

Angels? Maybe he should be a patient at Stryker... What was he going on about? I bet this is a test.

"You are named Amitiel for a reason. As I tried saying, I am Buer. We are quite famous you know," he chuckled trying to lighten the mood.

I stared at him in complete confusion. I kept coming back to the word Angel.

"I am doing an awful job at this!" Bow cried out in frustration, his aura turning a murky gray.

"Are you trying to tell me that I am an Angel or something?" His head sprung up. "I've always known that I was different, but this sounds ridiculous. You know that, right?"

"I'm sure it does. It is a relief you were able to understand where I was headed. Miss Ami, the world is more than you believe it to be. Angels are real. You and I are real…"

"You seem to know a lot about me. Do you know me?" I was testing him. I knew he did from his thoughts.

"You are Amitiel, the Angel of Truth. Your gifts should be unique to your calling. I am Buer; I was an Angel of Morals, Ethics, and Virtues."

"I'm not mistaken, you said *was*, as in past tense. Are you no longer an Angel?"

Bow did not answer my question. In fact, it was as if a light bulb switched off inside of him. Completely evasive, he gestured to his watch claiming we'd better get something to eat because it was almost time to head back.

I appeased him by not throwing a fit and demanding answers. Truth be told, I had plenty to process already from our tense conversation in the Church, and lunch did sound nice.

✝

Being outside of the Church now seemed surreal. Bow had made all the appropriate comments during our lunch and short drive back, but I knew his mind was lost in other thoughts. When we arrived at Stryker, he promptly walked me to my room, gently caressed my cheek, and kissed me before leaving. It felt nice being in the solitude of my bedroom. The information I learned was life altering. I needed to think.

It was out of character for me to venture anywhere other than Temperance's office during the day. There was just no getting around the awful human contact involved, until Bow shattered my quiet world with the A bomb.

From the moment Bow divulged that I was an Angel, I realized the truth he spoke. I knew there had to be a way to control my gifts. I just had to practice. I felt my power pulse through me, giving me an idea. I needed to paint, and I was not going to let the world stand in my way any longer.

The corridor was fairly empty. Just a few nurses writing notes on charts, an orderly playing solitaire at his desk, and Temperance was heading straight for me looking more runway model than Doctor. The way she looked in her black pencil skirt, and her amethyst colored blouse made every male on the floor turn their head and gawk.

I couldn't help but wonder if she knew I was an Angel. Was she? Temperance had claimed responsibility for me when no one else would.

Bow had said that they've known each other for years, and that she meant for our relationship to occur. I had to ask her, and now was my opportunity.

"Hello, Ami. Where are you headed? I don't usually see you out of your room in the day," Temperance said cheerfully.

"I was headed to find you actually," I lied. "Could I speak with you about something important please?"

"Of course you can. Let's head to my office."

I followed Temperance silently, holding my questions for the right moment. I could sense that she knew I was happy. It pleased her. I found it easy to control the flow of information I received, now that I knew it wasn't just happening to me, but rather that it was a part of me.

"Is everything alright?" She asked once I had taken a seat in her office.

"I'm quite well actually. I need to know something rather important though."

Temperance nodded.

"How long have you known that I'm different?" Holding my hand up I continued, "Let me rephrase, How long have you known that I am not bat-shit crazy?"

"From the moment you walked through the doors, Amitiel. Of course I know who you are, and that you are not crazy," She replied matter-of-factly. "Guarding you is my destiny. I take that very seriously."

"Bow and I didn't get to finish our conversation. I know that there is so much more to know. Why didn't *you* tell me?"

"Telling you about your past and about your true self is Bows destiny, and we must not interfere with another's destiny," she said wagging her finger. "I am sure he will tell you everything when the time is right."

Temperance moved toward the door, giving me the hint that it was time to go. She could not tell me anything without interfering with his destiny. I followed her to the door and left for the art room.

I heard the whispers when I entered the art room, but with some concentration I no longer heard the thoughts behind them. *Ah success*, I thought. I grabbed a blank canvas and my supplies from the cubby. I claimed the window by the corner to paint. I began by examining my finished pieces that hung from the wall, trying to find inspiration. They were all of an Angel. It was the same Angel, just with different scenes, different poses, and even different themes. I had an epiphany; subconsciously I must have known my true past and identity all along!

My identity is something I will come to understand. For now, I remain as Ami. One day that is bound to change, and with that transformation the Angel of truth will be resurrected. I have faith.

Dreamland

Most people have heard of Heaven, where those who are righteous are rewarded, and Hell, where those who are wicked are damned. That must make Stryker Memorial Hospital purgatory.

The day finally ended. I was pleased to find the outside hallway in silence. It made the new found space in my head all the more destitute, and pleasing. I took a shower to relax. I let the hot water run over my body in comfort. I had learned a lot about myself today. What I truly needed was some sleep. Sleep can cure anything. Finishing my shower, I went straight for my favorite soft blue pajamas and crawled into bed. I found myself asleep before my head even hit the pillow.

†

Peonies are my favorite flowers. I flitted about the large entryway admiring the fresh bunch I had in my arms. They were a beautiful soft pink, my favorite color. The credenza by the front door had an elegant crystal vase waiting for them. I felt the urge to make sure the flowers were just right. When I was pleased with their look, I retired to the reading room. I found my collection of poems composed by Edgar Allen Poe, and began to read my favorite piece out loud:

A dream

A wilder'd being from my birth
My spirit spurn'd control,
But now, abroad on the wide earth,
Where wand'rest thou my soul?

In visions of the dark night
I have dreamed of joy departed-
But a waking dream of life and light
Hath left me broken-hearted.

And is not a dream by day
To him whose eyes are cast
On things around him with a ray
Turned back upon the past?

That holy dream-that holy dream,
All the world were chiding,
Hath cheered me as a lovely beam
A lonely spirit guiding.

What though that light, thro' misty night,
So dimly shone afar-

> What could there be more purely bright
> In truth's day-star?

"Beautiful isn't it?" I said turning to my love. "Buer dear, did you hear me? The poem is lovely, is it not?"

"I find it rather tiresome, sweet Amitiel. Could you find one perhaps about love?" He asked.

"My silly, Buer. How I love your sullen moods. Why the poem is about love, and beauty."

"No beauty could ever compare to you," He cooed in the sweetest of manner.

"The sun is a glorious creation. The warm lick of her rays as you bask in her radiance is quite soothing. I do love our afternoons together, my Buer." I whispered to him, enticing him to lay with me upon the sofa. "Won't you join me, my love?"

He could not refuse me anything. Buer's warm embrace was even more Heavenly than the suns warmth. He gently caressed my cheek while gazing into my eyes. He found a stray curl out of place on my neck, and placed it behind my ear. His touch made me shiver in delight.

Buer undid each button on my dress slowly. Once off, he stroked my back and pulled me closer and closer until we were one. When our bodies collided we made music. Pale pink wings exploded from my back, creating a stunning glow. Buer took a moment to revel in their beauty. Smiling, he flexed his arms out and launched his dark blue wings from his sculpted back in one illustrious movement. He was glorious.

†

Being knocked abruptly from my dream, I found myself tangled in a mess of covers with a deep ache emanating from my shoulder blades. Quickly untangling myself, I tore the covers off and pulled off my soft blue velour jacket. My hands blindly searched the skin on my back for the cause of pain. When my fingers came up empty I dashed to the wall and threw on the light. Standing shirtless before the mirror I saw them; two puckered pink scars where my wings should be.

Panic stricken, I realized I needed Bow, and I needed him now. The clock on my bedside table read 5:23. I would have to wait for hours. I knew that I wouldn't make it that long, so with a deep breath I closed my eyes and began to find the space he occupied in my head. When I was sure I had a hold on it, I quietly sent him a message: 'I need you. Please come, I need you now.' I wrapped my jacket back around me and sat on the bed hoping and praying my gifts worked two ways, and that Bow would get my message.

Less than an hour later Bow charged into my room full speed. He found me on my bed curled in a tense ball. Bow rushed to my side, worry coloring his features. He must have come straight here because he was still in his pajamas. His fitted white t-shirt accentuated his firm torso, and gray sweat pants hung low on his waist – his hair was disheveled leaving me to think he was tossing and turning. There were bags under his eyes from exhaustion.

"You came," I said throwing myself at him. I needed to feel the strength and support his arms provided.

"I came because you called. I heard your voice so clear in my mind... I thought you were in my room. How did you do that?" He stroked my cheek tenderly trying to decipher my expression.

With a contented sigh, I responded, "I think I am getting this whole 'Angel' thing down." My vision still lingered in my head. The memories of him touching my body made me yearn for him now. I nuzzled him close, and softly kissed his neck whispering, "Thank you."

"Ami, listen to me," he said pulling me an arms distance away. "Even I cannot send telepathic messages. I want to know how you did it."

"Ever since you told me about who I am, I realized I could manage it. You know, control the voices and the information I get. I could focus, and even find peace. I hear you in my head, silly," I laughed ruffling his already messed up hair. "You have your own space in my head. So I found that space and called you. Is that wrong?"

"No. It just means we are even more connected than I anticipated we'd be. What else can you do, Ami?"

"Why is this so important?"

"It might help me understand why a snatcher was after you on the pier the other day. Please, just tell me."

"First, I want to know what exactly a 'snatcher' is and does, but I suppose it can wait. I assume you want to know the extent of my powers first, correct?"

"Yes."

"Well, I'm able to hear other people's thoughts. Until yesterday, it was a constant flow of information. Not just from anyone, but those I am familiar with. I can sense emotions. I feel them as if they are my own. Then, there is the aura thing."

"What?" Bow interrupted holding up his palm for me to pause and explain.

"You know, auras. I can see them. It helps me sense emotions and to decipher the truth in people's words or actions. It is entirely subjective though. I got a book on it once, when I was twelve. I almost have the color chart mesmerized."

Bow was nervous. He placed me back on the bed, and started to pace the room. Noises were beginning to come from the hallway. Bow peeked outside, then shut the door and locked it.

"I need to think," he mumbled.

I am not sure whether he was speaking to me, or himself, so I let him sort it out.

"Listen to me, Ami, snatchers are dangerous. You wanted me to explain who snatchers are and what they do… Well, they are demons sent by Lucifer to snatch the Fallen."

"How do you know this?"

"I'm not proud of my past, but for a while, I hunted demons. Do you remember the other day at the diner when I told you that I liked to hunt?"

"Yes, but you didn't clarify! I was picturing Bambi!" I exclaimed

"Well, like I said, I am not proud. I was mentally misguided for awhile," he muttered.

I decided that it wasn't important at the moment, and got back to topic. "What are the Fallen?" I prodded, my previous curiosity returning about the fear stricken way he said it.

"*We* are the Fallen, you and I. I am sure there are others too, but you are my priority. The snatchers have found you. They've come to collect. The man on the pier is just the beginning. You need to understand that when Lucifer wants something, he gets it, period." A shadow passed over his features when he mentioned the name Lucifer.

"That man, the snatcher, he knows I'm here. Bow, he knows I live here!" His face went pale in shock. "He almost ran me down to get on the elevator the day we went out to lunch. He must have come looking. Oh my God, what do we do?" Fear gripped me tight.

"Why did you call me this morning?" He asked suddenly.

My dream was ancient history, the danger of snatchers occupying my attention. I didn't forget though, how could I.

"I had a dream. It was a beautiful dream, Bow. I wanted to stay there forever. I need to show you something, please turn around."

While his back was to me, I slipped off my jacket and covered my breasts, turning so that my back was to him. "You can look now," I called.

I wish I could have seen his face. The onslaught of emotions that I felt crippled me to tears. It took me a moment to realize that they were his emotions that I was feeling. Bow traced the scars with a tenderness that touched my soul. My skin cooled in response. It provided me with a soothing relief from the pain I felt... *I had wings, and I had lost them.*

"You said that you had a dream?"

"Yes, I dreamed of us, a different version of us, however. One from long ago..."

"It is very rare for our kind to receive dream messages. Dreamland is forbidden to the Fallen. God must have been sending you a message." He spoke sullenly. "Are you alright? Does it hurt?"

"I feel better now that you've come. The pain I feel is much more than physical. I feel loss. I lost them, Bow. They were a part of me, and I lost them," I wept.

Bow began to caress me the way he did in my dream. His hands comforting me wherever they touched. He dried my tears. He could not refuse me anything, even now. He tenderly kissed my cried out eyes, the tip of my nose, my cheeks, and finally my lips.

Our kiss washed away any lingering fear and pain that I had. Bow was what I needed. He gently helped me put my jacket back on, covering my scars. During the tender kiss we shared, I felt him become a part of my soul. We were now, for better or worse, bound to one another.

"I have something to show you," he said, taking off his shirt. He turned around, arms tense at his sides, his hands clenched into fists.

Bows back revealed two scars identical to mine. The ridged pink lines were healed, but still looked painful. Without thinking much, I began to outline them with my fingertips. Bow trembled at my touch as if he was not expecting it on his back. Goosebumps covered his flesh, changing the once pink scars to lavender. He moaned at the pleasure my touch brought.

"They are beautiful. *You* are beautiful. I love you," I said as soft as a whisper.

Bow turned to face me. He cradled my face in his strong hands and replied, "As I love you."

Bow sat next to me on the bed and held me until breakfast. I used my new found restraint to suppress hearing his thoughts. With how close we have become, I felt it would be a violation of his trust.

We planned on seeing Temperance after we ate. When the time was more appropriate, Bow used my bathroom to clean up, and headed to the lounge to check in. He was on duty today.

I took his absence as an opportunity to ready myself for the day. I could only imagine what would be in store. I needed some normalcy. So I took care making my bed, gently folding the sheets and duvet just right. Once satisfied, I found it appropriate to open the window wide and check the weather. It was warm and sunny. I stood there for a moment taking a few deep breaths of fresh air. It did the trick and cleared my mind.

Thanks to Temperance I had several pieces of clothing to choose from. A warm day like this had me reaching for my white wrap-a-round dress. It hugged every curve my body had to offer. I decided to leave my hair down and placed a few rhinestone pins by my temples to hold the hair out of my face. There was a pair of gold sandals in my closet that completed the look perfectly. Even if my insides were a mess, I felt that I looked beautiful.

I was in the bathroom brushing my teeth and tending to my make-up when Bow reentered my room. At first I didn't hear him. I was too busy bopping back and forth and singing to myself. He startled me by clearing his throat. I jumped and giggled. Bow stood in the doorway to the bathroom smiling. He had changed his clothes and brought us some breakfast.

"You look happy, my dear Amitiel."

"I think it is wise to dress the way you want to feel. I look good," I said posing, "So I feel good."

Bow set down the breakfast tray and gave me a genuine hug, "You make me feel good."

"Did you see Temperance?"

"Yes, I filled her in on our snatcher friend. After we are done eating we're going to meet up, and figure out what to do about your safety. We must keep you from harm."

"What about you, Bow? You're a part of the Fallen. You need to be kept safe too!" I exclaimed.

"I am not the one the snatcher wants. He wants you. After you explained your gifts to me earlier, it got me thinking. You have more abilities than any Angel I have ever known. I think you are the key." further.

I sat there baffled, "What do you mean I am 'the key'?" I pushed using my fingers to make air quotes.

"In the beginning of time there was a revolt in Heaven. This was back before you and I had ever fallen. God wanted to grace the Earth with humans. Being the Angel of Truth, you expressed your concerns. Foreseeing all of the problems and destruction humans could create with free will, you took a stand," he said adoringly.

"I stood up to God?" Disbelief colored my tone.

"Yes you did. Only you were punished for it. God thought human beings were useful, that all lessons could be taught through living a human experience. You did not choose to fall, Amitiel. God pushed you."

Bow may have been present, but his mind was lost in the past. He was reliving the loss he experienced when I vanished. His face showed an array of sorrow to black fury. He felt betrayed by God.

"I could not stand for it. Once you were gone I chose to follow Lucifer, but by doing so, I chose to fall. God can do many things, Amitiel, but he cannot take away anyone's free will. I could not live a day in Heavens glory without you, the purest of souls, by my side."

I caressed his cheek smiling at the sacrifice he made. He loved me, who knows for how long. He chose me over Heaven.

"Where have you been? How did you even find me?" I asked.

"Temperance found me."

I knew he was hiding something. His aura was flickering red. I did not want to resort to entering his mind and finding the truth on my own. Out of respect he needed to tell me.

"Where?" I demanded.

Bow looked down and his shoulders sagged in defeat. He took a deep breath, and raised his head. His eyes searched mine, fervently looking for forgiveness.

Finding the love and trust he seemed to be probing for, Bow held my hands tightly and confessed, "Hell."

Broken-hearted

Anguish tore through me. I felt as if my heart were breaking. This time it was not only Bows emotions I was feeling. 'Hell'. The word held little to no meaning to me, Ami the girl, but to Amitiel the Angel of Truth, the word was quite profound.

Bows head sank in disgust, and silent tears streamed down his beautiful face. I hesitantly reached forward and stroked his hair. The overwhelming grief he felt was enough to melt me. I instantly grabbed him, and pulled him close to my chest, his ear resting just above my heart. I let the steady beat of my heart calm and reassure him of my love.

"Everyone makes mistakes, Bow," I whispered in comfort still stroking his hair.

"You were what gave me meaning in my existence. When you were gone, I felt as if I could no longer go on."

"Dry your tears, hush now. I am not one to judge. My love is yours regardless of the choices you made in my absence. I may not know much about us and who we once were, but

I will tell you that as the Angel of Truth I am a good judge of one's character. I do not question you, your love, or your loyalty, Buer. Not one bit." I pulled his head up to look in his eyes. I smiled and kissed him with unreserved passion.

"You are my heart," he said tenderly. "Once we figure out your safety I will explain so much more to you. You need to know everything. I want you to know everything."

"Temperance I'm sure is waiting. Are you ready?"

With no hesitation, Bow raised from the bed glowing a bright orange. It took a large amount of courage for him to admit his sin. He took my hand confidently, and we headed for Temperance's office. The futures uncertainties made the walk down the corridor to her office seem that much longer. The only thing I was certain about held my hand securely, keeping my feet firm on the ground.

"I've been expecting the two of you," Temperance said as she greeted us at the door to her office.

"Thank you for seeing us, Temperance. We need your guidance," I explained taking a seat on her sofa with Bow.

"Guidance, I see," she said with a smile playing at her lips. "Guidance is my specialty, darling. I am after all, your Guardian Angel."

By this point, I felt immune to the bizarre. In the three days that I have been back at Stryker,

I have met my soul-mate, been stalked by a snatcher, found out that I am an Angel, and that I may or may not be a 'key' to who the Hell knows what. If I wasn't already deemed insane by the state, I am sure I would be now. Who would believe this?

Finding an inner calm I responded by shrugging my shoulders. "You have always been there. I suppose it makes sense."

"Bow was right," Temperance commented. "You are taking this quite well."

We all quietly laughed at the sheer insanity we were experiencing.

"So about the guidance... What do we do about the snatcher that is after me? Oh, and also why is he after me? I remember something about a key?"

"First off, you and Bow are perfectly safe here. I choose Stryker for a reason. No one can access this floor without clearance from me," she assured tapping her pencil to her temple with a smug look. "You are here, in the Psych Ward for protection. Please understand it has never been about insanity, Ami. I had to keep you in the dark for your protection. You could not be told the truth until the right time."

"Right time meaning, when you found Bow."

"Yes, you are correct," she replied nervously.

"Don't worry," I told her. "I know about you finding him in Hell."

"I already told her," Bow explained. "She is doing her best to not listen to my thoughts, and I sensed her discomfort. I love her too much to have her worry."

Smiling, Bow reached for my chin and brought my face to his for a quick kiss. I blushed deeply.

"Very well then. To answer the rest of your questions, the snatcher is after you because you, my sweet Amitiel, are *the key to salvation*." She spoke matter-of-factly., as if this were common knowledge. "I'm sure you are beginning to understand that you are quite different from the rest of the Fallen, in more ways than one. Your gifts are much more advanced than Bows, or even mine, and not to state the obvious, but you did not fall from choice. You were punished, for lack of a better word."

"Bow briefly explained that to me."

"Did he explain what that means for you?"

"I honestly didn't know how to explain that to her," he interposed.

"I see. Let me see if I can," she said, pausing a moment to think. "There are many kinds of Angels, all with different gifts, talents, purposes, and destinies. For instance, I am a Guardian Angel. I guard pure souls from harm, and provide guidance when those under my protection seek it."

It made sense that Temperance was a Guardian Angel. I always thought of her as pure and kind hearted.

"You and Bow are a bit difficult to explain. Your talents are rare. You, Ami, are the protector of truth, and Bow, the protector of morality. Your talents are rare because you are the originals. Do you understand what I am telling you?" She asked.

"I believe so."

"The connection you share with each other is uncommon. It was never meant to happen. I guess you could say that you two were Gods left and right hand Angels. Think about it, what good was morality without honesty? The fact that your souls connected changed everything. It essentially changed Gods plan."

"Is that why Ami was sent to this God awful forsaken place?" He asked outraged.

"Calm down," I quietly reproved.

"I cannot speak for God, Bow. I will not make assumptions as to why things happen. It is not my place. However, I will tell you that it speaks volumes that the love you share was not meant to happen, and yet it still is."

Bow and I were still holding hands. We turned to each other and looked deeply into the other's eyes. I could tangibly feel the bond we shared. It did speak volumes.

Without looking away from him I asked Temperance, "So how am I different? What makes me the key?"

"That is a rather easy question to answer. You are *the key* simply because God made it that way. He chose you, Amitiel. What may seem like a chastisement, I'm sure has a reason for being. You have a destiny quite different than most. It was foreseen long ago that corruption would destroy the earth..."

Frustrated, I interrupted, "Yes. I foresaw that apparently before I was so rudely pushed." I felt like we were getting nowhere. I truly hated being spoken to like a preschooler.

"It was also predicted that a savior would grace earth and return the lost souls. The savior in doing so would return Gods creation, the earth and humanity, back to peace and civilization."

"So I'm like what, the savior?"

"Through your love, and your innocence, you have the power to redeem the Fallen. Your destiny is to return the Fallen to God. You are *the key* to their salvation, so yes, you are the savior I refer to. It is your destiny."

"So you're telling me I'm supposed to find the Fallen and offer them a chance to go back? I don't even fully understand where I'd be sending them, or how to guide them. I'm afraid you lost me, Temperance," I complained.

"I know this situation seems like a lot to deal with, but you are not alone. You have me. We'll figure this out together," Bow pointed out.

"Bow is right, Ami. Who is to say how large Gods plan is. Does it stop when you fall? Or is this all just a continuation of His plan? One can only guess. What I do know is that the two of you are greatly needed. Angels were never meant to roam the Earth. You need to save them, and set it right."

This was a lot to process. I barely feel accountable for myself, and now I am faced with a responsibility that far outweighs the capabilities of a seventeen year old. Am I seventeen? How far does this go back? The earth is really old, shouldn't I be? I think I'm getting a headache. I rested my head in my hands. This is all too much.

"Amitiel, we appear to be safe here. I'm sure our mission can wait a few days. You must need time to absorb what we've told you. How are you feeling? You didn't eat much breakfast. Would you like to get some fresh air?" Bow was worried. He began stroking my back in comfort.

"It's a lot to handle," I admitted in all honesty. "I feel morosely unqualified to handle the salvation of God only knows how many lost souls."

I literally felt the weight of the world on my shoulders. I needed to get away from here, from Temperance, from Angel business, even from

Bow. Quietly I excused myself and left. I'm not sure where I planned to go. Anywhere but here sounded nice. The last image I had was of the hurt look on Bows face as I pushed his hand away when exiting the room.

†

I don't drive. I've never had the chance to learn. So my options were limited when it came to escape. Since Stryker was located in the heart of the city, it did not make much sense to leave the grounds. The art room was undoubtedly crowded at this time of day, and I didn't feel like concentrating on controlling my gifts. That left either my room, or the roof. I chose the roof. Bow would check my room, and I couldn't bear facing him now.

The roof contained a garden with a relaxing man-made waterfall. There were lovely stone benches that lined the outdoor safe-haven bearing plaques in honor of the hospitals donors. I have only been there a few times, usually for lunch with Temperance, but I loved it. I needed peace, and the garden provided that.

I felt relief the moment the elevator bells dinged at the top, leaving me to exit into the garden. I found a bench in the shade and sat down. Meditating was never my strong suit, but I decided to give it a try. Racking my brain, I found a quiet corner. Closing my eyes I concentrated on the quiet, and took steady deep breaths. The only thing I focused on was the feeling of the air as it entered my nose, went down my air pipes, filled my lungs, and the relief it brought when released.

Peace swirled around me, filling me and completing me. I felt empowered. I no longer felt the ache of a broken heart. I no longer felt the weight of the world. I felt like me, the old me, just Ami the girl. I continued my deep breathing, only opening my eyes to look around the garden and admire the flowers in bloom.

This truly was a lovely place. Trellises lined the edges of the roof, with blooming tea roses. Splashes of pink, white, and yellow covered them. There was a cobblestone path that weaved its way through the lush green grass that surrounded a young ash tree. The tree provided shade for most of the stone benches. You could hear the soft trickle of the waterfall in the corner, and the songbirds that came to feed from the birdfeeders hanging in the tree. This was a place made entirely out of peace.

When the sun began to set, throwing beautiful colors across the sky, I got up to stretch. I felt stiff from the hard bench. My head was still quiet. Through the meditation, I began to stop focusing on all the problems, and just accept what is. It made me feel better. I needed this.

The bell to the elevator startled me. My senses were alerted to the unseen company I had on the roof. I'd like to say that blind panic didn't overcome me, but it did. I had to remember that I was a target. I couldn't just call out, 'hey, who's there?' like some stupid teenage girl about to get killed in a horror movie. I had to remain quiet and take note of my surroundings.

Every noise and every footstep seemed to be amplified inside the quiet space in my head. It was a feeling I was not used to. Right away I noted the timid steps the unknown person made. It did not seem like someone who knew where they were going. They seemed to be searching for something, maybe even searching for... *me*. I didn't have much time, soon the sun would finish setting and I would be left in the dark. I had to act.

I needed a vantage point where I could see, and not be seen. I decided that short of climbing the tree, hiding behind it would be appropriate. I mentally kicked myself that today was the day I decided to wear a white dress, and sandals. I'd be no good in a fight if it were a snatcher up here. I sent Bow a silent message of help. I just prayed he received my silent plea, like he did that last one.

My time was up. The intruder found me crouched behind the tree. It was not Temperance or Bow as I had secretly been hoping. This man was someone I had never met before, but inherently I knew. This man was a snatcher, I was sure of it.

I stood up out of my crouch and faced him. He was quiet, just tilting his head to the side as if appraising me, his prize. He wore all black, right down to the trench coat. He was old, and thin. Everything about him screamed, DANGER! DANGER! Not sure of what to do, I spoke.

"So you've found me. May I ask who I have the pleasure of meeting?"

The wicked man smiled his creepy smile and grumbled under his breath. He had no plans of telling me anything, so I continued.

"Well Frank, may I call you Frank? I feel I must call you something if we're to speak."

He nodded in assent.

"Well Frank, I feel as though you have wasted your trip. You see I have no intention of going with you. I have work to do, work that does not involve your boss."

My new buddy Frank just laughed and licked his lips. *Ewww gross!* He started to move towards me. Not knowing what else to do I backed up and firmly planted my feet, attempting to brace myself for whatever this disgusting creepy demon had planned. That is when I felt it…

The pain was excruciating. It sent me reeling forward. When I was able to catch my breath and stand up I realized that I had changed. Something magnificent happened. My wings had been returned bringing my memory, and all the power and ancient wisdom I had lost in the fall back to me. The lavish pale pink shimmer was a sight. I stood confidently, and flexed them outward.

Now it was time for Frank to stumble. And stumble he did — backwards. The sight of my power shone through every flap my wings took. He was scared, and yet in awe of the beauty I possessed. With a blink of an eye, Frank vanished. Black dust hovered in his wake.

Just then the elevator bell dinged again. Temperance and Bow came charging full force through the doors as they opened, both coming to a shuddering halt when they saw me. The look of wonder was present on their faces. They stood before me mouths gaping. My wings spread wide, moving and reacting to my every whim.

I smiled at them and let loose a peal of laughter. This moment, was my moment. I stood before my guardian and mate and proudly declared, "I remember."

Revelations

Things had definitely changed in the last twenty-four hours. My Guardian Angel Temperance and my beloved Buer had found me on the roof. To their surprise I had found my own inner salvation and got my wings back. What a trip that was!

Needing privacy to discuss what happened on the roof before their arrival, we decided that after a good night's sleep we should meet in the garden the next morning. I awoke feeling truly happy for once in my life.

It was a warm Tuesday morning in May. The sun shined bright in the clear blue sky. The old me would have done her best to sneak off to the beach. The new me, however, finally understood the first seventeen years of my life. I find it amazing how one shared secret can shed new light on everything. I now saw things differently. Perhaps that was indicative to me being different now that my wings had returned. All I knew was that I had a lot of work ahead of me finding and redeeming the Fallen.

After breakfast, I showered and dressed in a rush. With the day being so lovely, I chose to wear another sundress. This one was pure white and girly. Temperance bought it for me long ago, and until this morning I had never put it on. When I thought of myself now, I thought of my pink wings, and that made me feel beautiful and feminine.

I practically floated on cloud nine up to the roof where I was to meet Bow and Temperance. I sang under my breath and danced to my own beat. Twirling fluttered my dress into a bell. I knew if I looked in a mirror I'd be glowing. The look on Bows face confirmed that as he scooped me into his arms. Damn he looked good this morning. Decked in army fatigue shorts, a fitted black t-shirt and white k-Swiss sneakers, he looked like an all American boy next door. Thank God that boy was mine.

"Good morning, love," I said with a huge genuine smile appraising him.

"Good morning to you." Bow kissed me tenderly making me blush.

"Shall we get started, you two love birds?" Temperance chimed in. She was also alight. I could tell that my happiness made her feel joyful.

Bow and I both laughed quietly and took our seats on the soft yellow picnic blanket that was spread out under the ash tree.

"Sure thing," I replied as I got myself settled. I grabbed a handful of almonds that Temperance set out for a snack. Bow politely handed me a glass of tea.

"Where should we start?" He asked.

"I suppose the first question to ask is obvious. How am I to know where to look for the Fallen? It is not as if the Fallen are listed in the phone book— Wait," I held up my hand, "Are they?" I asked only half serious.

"If you mean have they adapted, and do they lead human lives, I'm sure some do," Temperance replied smoothing out her long royal blue skirt over her side swept legs.

"Some I'm afraid are going to be a bit harder to find than that. Quite a few I'd venture chose to follow Lucifer," Bow added.

"Fan-freakin-tastic," I mumbled. Couldn't anything in my life be easy? Not only did it seem I was going to have to scour the earth, but it appeared as though I might have to take a trip to Hell too. I'm sure Lucifer will just love that. I was determined not to let this affect my mood. I was finally happy, and planned on staying that way.

Bow chucked at my expression and mussed my hair. That did the trick. My lighter mood from earlier returned.

I took a sip of my tea and began, "So, if I'm to travel to Hell to redeem some of the Fallen, how am I to return?"

It was Temperance who spoke up, "I would imagine that same way you enter."

"We all know Lucifer wants me badly. I doubt he'll just let me visit the underworld and steal his minions."

"She's right. Lucifer won't just let her in and out, Temperance. What would you suggest?"

"While I do not condone you going to the underworld, I dare say that it must happen in order for you to be successful. You should be delicate about it though, Ami, no attitude. I would recommend that you appeal to Lucifer's kind side," Temperance said grimly. "Don't look at me like that, Amitiel. For Heaven's sake you can be nice," she joked, "…and I know what you're thinking, and yes, he does have one."

"So, I'm to what? Call him up and ask him to coffee to discuss this rationally?" I sarcastically joked.

"Exactly."

"What?!?"

"Wait, wait, wait, back up. You want Ami to contact him? You think we can trust Lucifer to hand the Fallen over? Just like that?" Bow questioned alarmingly.

"Bow, did I once infer that this task would be easy?" Temperance asked him perturbed. "I simply said that if Ami is to go she must speak with Lucifer directly."

I had never seen Temperance irritated before. Her beautiful face wasn't meant to display such emotion.

Bow, sensing his misstep, apologized. "I am sorry for directing my anger towards you, dear friend."

Instantly her sour mood dissipated. Temperance took more goodies from her basket and laid them before us to eat.

I was reeling from their little spat. I had just grabbed a banana from her goodie pile when Temperance took my arm and spoke seriously, "You must remember that while he once was your equal in Heaven, he is your superior in Hell."

"Excuse me?"

"Don't you think that Lucifer would harm her if she threatened the Underworld?" His concern was building.

While she was deep in thought I finished my snack, and poured another glass of tea for myself. If you set aside what we were speaking about, this was a rather nice picnic.

"I am not sure my guidance will help in this situation," Temperance admitted.

"It appears the safest way for me to get close to Lucifer is to get myself caught," I stated, silencing Bow with a simple glare. "I know it is dangerous, but it seems to be the only way. The Fallen that reside in the Underworld should be my priority. Everything after that will seem easy," I finished trying to appease him and sound confident.

Bow was not convinced, but he didn't say one word. The raw anger and fear that flowed off of him was tangible. Even Temperance shifted her position uneasy.

"So it is settled then. I will go about my business, and when the snatchers come for me, I will go willingly," I surmised.

"It's dangerous," Bow stressed. "You must promise to keep yourself safe no matter what. I cannot afford to lose you. I need you, and the Fallen need you. Promise me?" Bow pled.

"Of course I do."

Bow and I were headed to see a movie. There was no sense in hiding if I wanted to be captured. I desperately needed to laugh.

"Let's laugh, eat popcorn, and try to relax tonight, okay?" He begged.

"Sounds like a plan." Bow laughed at my expression and bought two tickets for us.

We found ourselves fully loaded with popcorn, two monster size sodas, and licorice. Upon entering the theater, we grabbed two seats in an empty back corner. I settled into my seat enjoying the dark noisy theater. The movie hadn't started yet, leaving the patrons lively with enthusiasm. I snuggled close to Buer.

"Can you send me messages back? You know, when I send them telepathically to you, can you send them back?" I asked breaking our silence.

"That was out of the blue," he remarked. "Truthfully, I've never tried. I don't think so, but with how bonded we've become, who knows," he replied with a slight shrug.

I was extremely curious, so I closed my eyes, found the special spot I save for him in my mind, and sent, 'I love you' flooded with an embellishment of peonies I pictured in my mind. I must have startled him because he practically sprung from the theater seat, tossing popcorn everywhere. I couldn't help it, I laughed out loud.

"Did you like my message? I thought you could try to send one back. By the way, did you see the flowers? I was trying something new."

"I didn't jump from your message, though it was quite impressive." Then closing his eyes, he telepathically sent back, 'the snatchers have come; two rows in front of us to the left. Lucifer seems to have sent five of them.' Fierce panic colored his message. His aura flickered between a bright red for anger, and a murky gray riddled with sorrow.

I slowly rose from my seat and made my way for the exit. No way was I going to be making a scene here in the crowded theater. It took me over an hour last time to put my wings away.

They should come with an instruction manual. I'm just not sure how the moviegoers would interpret a real life Angel amidst them.

Bow followed me out, abandoning our snacks and good seats. Our one and only date was ruined. It certainly didn't take my good friend Frank long to report back to Lucifer about me. He must feel that extra reinforcements were necessary this time. Hence the five snatchers that staggered out behind us.

I quietly led everyone through the lobby and exited out the back doors of the theater that led to the empty alleyway.

"Why hello, boys," I greeted the snatchers condescendingly. "I believe you've come to collect me for your, how do I say... master."

The snatchers tossed a bevy of weird glances towards each other. The large one, who appeared at the head of their formation, seemed to be in charge.

With great confidence I ventured to speak only with him. "You there," I nodded towards him, "What is your name?"

He looked around as if he was mistaken that I intended to speak with him. Once the oaf figured it out, he responded, "You can call me Mac," he replied.

"Well, Mac, could you and your comrades escort me to your master?" I asked, flicking a gesture toward his dirty motley crew.

That did it, they all looked around confused. They thought it was a trick. Funny beings these snatchers are. I cannot fathom a read on them, or even see their auras. No question they'd be black. It was brutally clear that they are a very dense bunch of demons. Perhaps they'll need some provoking. I really should include my anxious lover in my plan to humiliate them.

I sent Bow a quiet telepathic message, 'follow my lead.' Instantly, he received it, and prepared for whatever I threw his way.

"Perhaps I didn't make myself clear, Mac," I declared with power. I extended my arms out to my sides and thrust my wings from my exposed back. Thank goodness my white dress left my back bare.

Bow shifted his weight back and forth nervously, his arms outstretched protectively. I stood, arms crossed looking bored. Mac and his motley crew didn't know what was going on. Perhaps they needed further invoking. I raised my left hand before me with my palm up, and envisioned a blue orb of light nestled into it. I'm not sure why, but instincts told me I had untapped powers.

Once envisioned, the blue orb appeared. I smiled with satisfaction. Mac looked terrified. Twirling the orb I reiterated a bit louder, "Mac dear, take me to your master… NOW."

Mac's once scared and dumbfounded expression turned cold, and he started to advance on me. Bow was not having it. He leapt in front of me to block Mac's approach. Now it was my turn to be scared. Bow was my heart, a part of my soul. I couldn't let him put himself in harm's way for me. I hurled the orb right at Macs head.

Bow stumbled back when the orb hit Mac. He spun and looked at me horror struck. I ignored his reaction, re-crossed my arms, and began to tap my foot. For God sakes, I didn't kill him. I merely froze him for a bit. I was strictly nonviolent, he knew that.

The motley crew stood there starring at the unmoving remains of their leader, Mac.

"I said, take me to your master. Do I need to be more clear?" I shouted, finding an inner source of anger.

The man to step forward from the bunch looked apprehensive at first, before he settled on a deep burning rage. He formed a slick black orb of his own and twirled it tauntingly at Bow.

"Should I damage your precious mate, Angel? Or should I send you a blaze?" The snatcher sneered.

Only he didn't wait for my answer, he had made one. The ominous snatcher flung his dark command straight at Bow. Thank God my Bow is quick. He dodged the black orb, letting it collide into the wall of stone behind us in a fiery crash.

Was that it then? His fire to my ice? I had to think fast. Soon innocent people would hear, and come to investigate the noise if this continued. Bow read my thoughts and stepped forward in surrender.

"Comrades, let's take this somewhere more appropriate, shall we? Perhaps my mate is correct. Would you fine soldiers take us to see Lucifer? He is an old friend of mine. We mean no harm," Bow concluded raising his hands up in further surrender.

Mac's crew remained focused. I may not be able to read them, but their expressions were clear. I raised my palm, and prepared to defend my love. Only the snatchers were faster. They began to fling their dark orbs at us with blinding speed. Bow instantly was in my head sending me a message, 'black magic not only wounds, but also can kill you, Amitiel! We must retreat!'

Bow flung all sorts of defensive shields before us, blocking an enormous deal of the onslaught. It wasn't enough though. Bow was growing weaker with each powerful hit his shield took on my behalf. I dug deep, extended both palms before me, and sent a wave of white energy at them, exerting everything I had within my tiny frame.

The force sent the remaining four of them reeling backwards, but only further pissed them off.

"Stop!" I commanded, and they did. "To Lucifer, please. I do not wish to harm you like your friend."

Bow took his place at my side, and held my hand further proving our commitment to stop fighting.

The same brave snatcher that spoke before decided to take charge and speak again. "I see you are strong, Angel. You'll simply go with us? It is not a trick?" He asked.

"No, it is not. I will not resist, if you concede and stop this wasteful fight. I need to speak with Lucifer. As it is, you came at a good time."

"What about your mate?" The snatcher inquired.

I stole a glance at Bow, who never seemed to release his shield. *Always my protector that dear boy*, I thought. "He'll remain on earth. I must go alone," I said stroking the back of Bows hand with my thumb in comfort.

I knew that the thought of me going with these losers hurt and scared Bow to his core, but as always he could deny me nothing. If this were what I chose, he would honor it. That much was clear. This was our opportunity. I needed to meet with Lucifer. I needed to find a way to free the Fallen from the Underworld.

I turned to Bow, "It's time to leave. Release your shield, and let me go, my love. I must go with them. You have been valiant in my defense. I love you and will return soon."

This had the snatchers laughing. They did not think I would be able to return. My, my, my how my exterior fools them. For I may look like Ami the ditzy teen, but my inner core is Amitiel, the illustrious Angel of Truth. These fools were barking up the wrong tree.

I kissed Bow and released his hand. I tucked my wings back in place. It was much easier this time, now that I knew what to do. Stepping forward to my escorts, I stole one last glance at Bow. Too bad it was not a memory I wished to keep. The horror on his face as the black fire clipped his shoulder was too much to bear.

Behind my back, the traitor snatchers thrust one last black orb upon our exit! There was no time to act. The snatchers had me in their grip, and we left the alley behind for a swirl of darkness.

Pain grappled my insides. Bow was wounded, and in need of me. I could feel his pain. I wanted to be back with him, to help him. It was a lost battle. We were on our way to Hell. I got my wish, a meeting with Lucifer.

The feeling of anguish almost caused a new fight, though I thought better as I was sure to lose on their turf. Settling on the only option I had, I sent Temperance a telepathic message containing the recent events, and Bows whereabouts. The message was tinged with pain, sadness, and fear for I knew not what I had gotten myself into.

Follow Ami's Hellbound journey in *Lost*

AVAILABLE NOW